Pops the Magic Taxi Visits Battersea

by

Fiona Kennedy

ISBN: 978-1-5272-2760-6

Printed by The Lavenham Press
www.lavenhampress.com
enquiries@lavenhamgroup.co.uk

Thanks to Roger Fletcher for illustrating
Judith Paskin for editing
Tuire Siiriainen for the finishing touches
Battersea Power Station for allowing access to their Media Library
Family and friends for editing, ideas and encouragement
Rett UK for the support given to Pops
For more information please visit www.rettuk.org
And my lovely Mum. x

They say 'There's a book in everyone.'

Well, to my surprise, there was one in me!

I am a mum and have been a London cabbie since 2001. I love my job. I love the city, the architecture, and I have the loveliest passengers.

It all started Christmas 2016. I was given a journal from my marvellous friend. On the cover it read 'For my great ideas.' Over the years I had told her about my inventions, none of which were really workable, to be honest. However, I noted the ones I could remember and just left them there in the book.

I was stuck in traffic in Park Lane one day when I suddenly had this idea of a story about a magic taxi. I wasn't sure how it was going to work, but I got my book out, wrote down the title and put it away (after stopping somewhere safe, of course!).

Several weeks later, I was travelling on a coach to the British Museum for a class visit, when we passed Battersea Power Station. It was a hive of activity; after many years of being vacant it was finally being renovated. I got the children to count the cranes.

Like a lot of London cabbies, I listen to BBC Radio London. I have heard presenter Jo Good say 'There's a book in everyone' on numerous occasions, but it had never stirred anything inside me before.

I had a lightbulb moment; everything came together. I had an idea for a book: that was the seed. The location, Battersea, was the earth. Finding out about London's past was the water and Jo was the sunshine. Something clicked in my head and a beautiful Poppy grew.

The magic taxi had to be called 'Pops.' One of my very best friends has a daughter who suffers from Rett syndrome, a rare neurological disorder affecting mainly females. Her name is Poppy but we call her 'Pops' for short.

I really hope you enjoy reading her first adventure.

Fiona

Dedicated to Alison, Mick, Dan and Pops

"Are you going to work today, Mum?" Joe asked.

"Not exactly. I'm going to look at a new taxi," said Mum. "Do you want to come with me?"

"Oh, yes please!" he replied.

"Always starts first time. Just needs a clean, that's all," said Al, the old taxi driver.

"I can help, Mum," Joe declared as he pulled at the overgrown weeds and poppies. "Please can you get it?" he begged.

"Well, it's not what I expected..." Mum pondered as she turned the key.

VROOM

LOOODON

"Hey! It really does start first time – I'd love to buy it!"

"That's great!" Al cheered.

"It's got a mind of its own," he shouted to them as they drove off.

The mechanic at the garage checked the taxi over.
Afterwards, everyone helped to give it a good clean.

"She was covered in poppies, so let's call her Pops!" Joe suggested.

"What a perfect name," Mum agreed.

"Welcome to the Painter family, Pops," said Joe. He gently patted the bonnet.

"Ah, that feels better," a voice said softly.

LOOODON

Every day, Mum collected Joe from school in her taxi.

"Can we go the long way home today, Mum?" Joe asked.
"I want to count cranes."

Joe watched the cranes **lifting,** the diggers **digging,** and the giant drills making holes in the ground.

"Six... seven... eight... nine!" Joe announced. "I love driving past Battersea Power Station. I wonder what it used to be like."

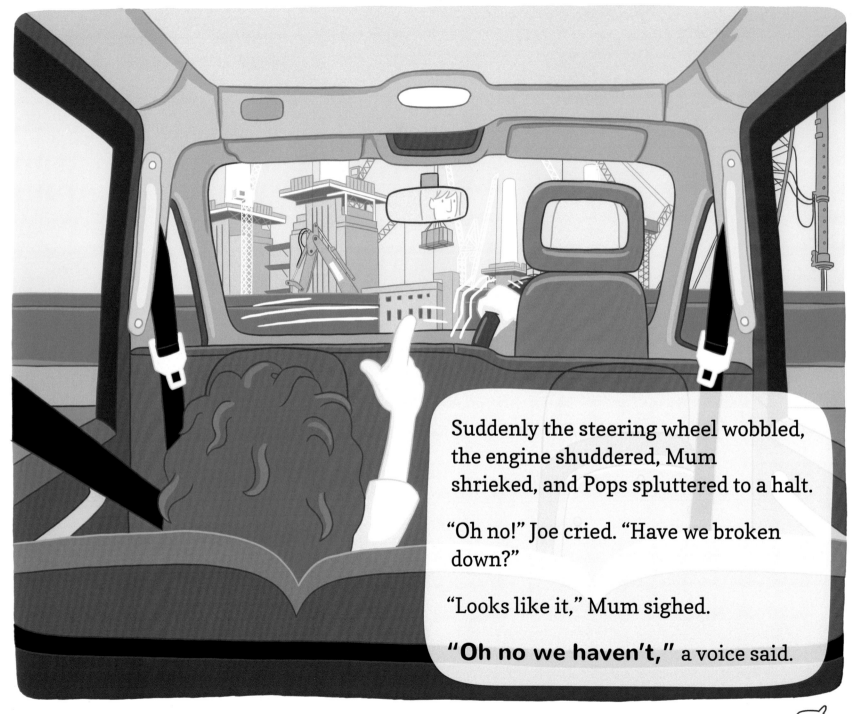

Suddenly the steering wheel wobbled, the engine shuddered, Mum shrieked, and Pops spluttered to a halt.

"Oh no!" Joe cried. "Have we broken down?"

"Looks like it," Mum sighed.

"Oh no we haven't," a voice said.

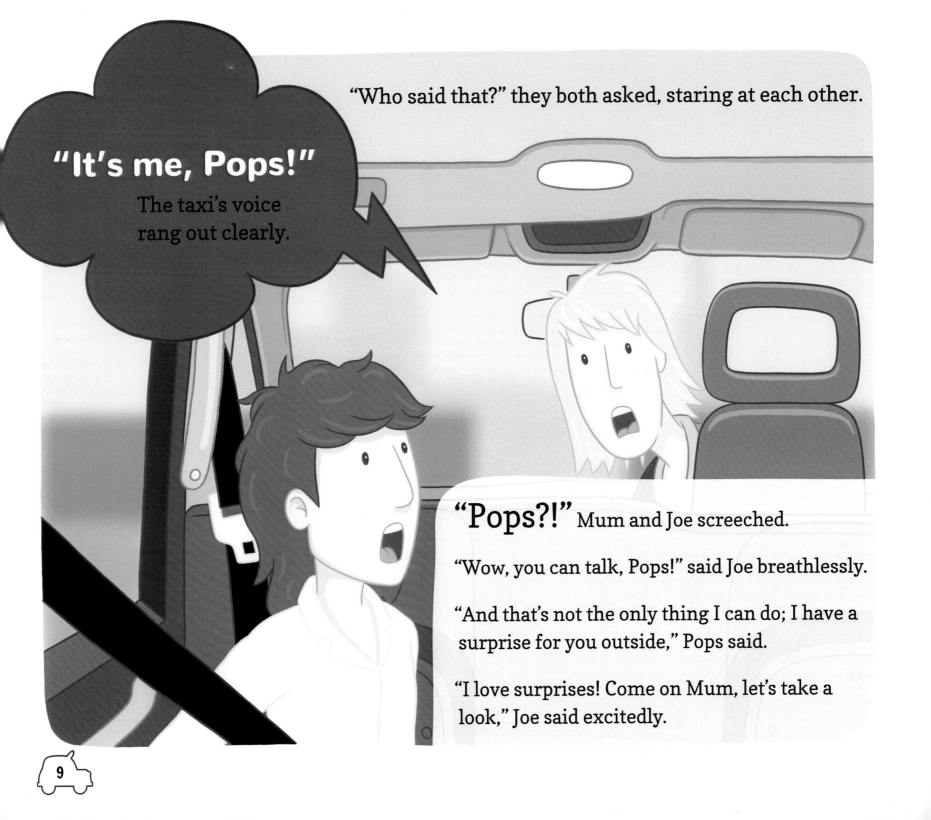

Mum and Joe got out of the taxi. All of the cranes, diggers and drills had disappeared and Battersea Power Station had come back to life.

"Let's go over there," Joe said, tugging on Mum's arm and pointing to a group of people.

"**Save** our trees! **Save** our paintings!" the crowd chanted over and over.

"May we take a look at your newspaper, sir?" Mum asked a gentleman next to her.

The gentleman handed it to Joe who took one look and gasped. "Mum, it's 1933! These people are worried that smoke from the Power Station will kill all the trees in the park and ruin all the paintings in the Tate Gallery."

Before he could continue, a scruffy black dog, just like Joe's dog, ran past him.

"Rover! Rover!" a little girl called out, sobbing. "My dog's run off! The dogs' home told me not to let him off the lead too soon," she cried.

"He's just run over there," said Joe. "What's your name?"

"It's Flo," she said, sniffing.

"Don't worry, Flo. I'm a good finder. You'll soon have him back."

Mum, Joe and Flo followed Rover into an open doorway in the Power Station, but he quickly disappeared.

Workers in overalls were waiting for a lift. Joe spotted paw prints on the steps and said, "He's gone up there!"

Joe and Flo raced off, taking two steps at a time, leaving Mum to chase after them.

Engineers were looking at dials, writing on clipboards, and turning switches.

Joe wanted to fiddle with the dials, but he decided he'd better not.

They couldn't see Rover, so they quietly crept towards a big window.

"That's where electricity is made," Joe said, looking down at a huge machine. "I learnt it at school, Mum."

"I am impressed!" she replied.

"There's Rover, sniffing the coal!" Joe shouted.

One of the engineers looked up. "Oi! What are you doing in the control room?"

"Quick! Let's grab Rover and get out of here," said Mum, rushing out of the door.

But where was Rover?

"He's gone again," sobbed Flo.

Joe looked around. "There he is! Oh no, he's on the conveyor belt and heading for the furnace!" he said.

Rover got **closer**

and **closer.**

"How do we stop it?" shouted Flo.

"We need to turn it off at the controls," Joe replied, running over to the buttons.

"Hurry!" Flo called out.

He paused. "Green, go. Red, stop," he whispered.

He pushed the red button with all his might.

Everything stopped and the furnace door shut.

Rover ran back along the conveyor belt and jumped down.

Rover raced towards Flo and jumped all over her.

"Thank you, Joe. You **really** are a good finder," she laughed and tried to brush the paw prints off her dress. We had better get out of here before we get into trouble."

"Have you got anything to eat, Mum? I'm really hungry," Joe asked.

"Why don't you come back with me to Battersea Park?" Flo suggested. "I was having a picnic by the boating lake before Rover ran off."

"Isn't everything covered in soot from the Power Station?" Joe asked her.

"No, that hasn't happened," Flo replied.

"How about the paintings in the Tate Gallery?" he said.

"They're fine too. My grandfather is an engineer at the Power Station. He cleans the chimneys to reduce the air pollution," Flo said with pride.

BEEP
BEEP

"Mum!" Joe shouted
excitedly. "Look, it's Pops!"

"Sorry, Flo. We won't be able to
come to your picnic; our taxi's
here," Mum said.

"Look after Rover," Joe told her.

"Will do! I'm going to train him.
Thank you for helping me!" she
said, smiling.

"How did you find us, Pops?" Joe asked as he got into the taxi.

"I always know where you are," Pops replied.

Pops's steering wheel wobbled and the engine shuddered. But Mum didn't shriek this time.

"That was so much fun! Pops is our magic taxi. Will she take us on another adventure one day?" asked Joe.

"I hope so," said Mum. "What do you say, Pops?"

"You try and stop me!"

Pops giggled.

The end, for now...

Before you go...

Did you knw...

Sir Giles Gilbert Scott designed the outside of Battersea Power Station. He also designed the outside of Tate Modern, and our classic red telephone boxes.

There were approximately 60 million bricks used to build Battersea Power Station.

When it opened it only had two chimneys; the other two were not finished until 1953.

Each chimney is 337 feet tall: that's the same as just over 23 double-decker buses stacked up on top of each other.

Locals and even King George V were worried that it was too big and everything around it would get covered in pollution from the chimneys.

Coal from Wales and the North East of England was brought in by train and ship; cranes would lift it onto a conveyor belt.

Once inside the Power Station, the coal was crushed into powder and burnt in large furnaces, which heated 160 million gallons of Thames river water. The boiling water created steam; this turned the turbine and spun the coil and made electricity.

The excess hot water was pumped under the Thames to Pimlico and used to heat homes.

The Power Station stopped producing electricity in 1983.

Battersea's new energy centre will provide heating and cooling for the whole development.

Tate Britain shows amazing British art from the year 1500 to today.

By 1935 the Tate had electric lights so more people could visit after dark.

Battersea Dogs and Cats Home has been on this site since 1871. Since then they have rescued, reunited and rehomed over 3.1 million cats and dogs.

RIVER THAMES

map by
Sophie
& Ellen

Rett UK
Support today, hope for tomorrow

Rett UK support Pops
(and many other families)
and Pops the Magic Taxi
supports Rett UK.

Pops
the
Magic
Taxi